Annabelle
the Drawing
Fairy

by Daisy Meadows

ORCHARD

www.rainbowmagic.co.uk

The Fairyland Palace

Bridge

Sara Sketchley's house

Rainspell

Island

Maze

Park

Carys's Jewellery Shop

Beach and Promenade

Jack Frost's
Ice Castle

Campsite

Girls'
tent

Market Square

Mimosa
Cottage

Pottery Hall

Sunshine
Cake Shoppe

Polly Painterly's Workshop

Jack Frost's Spell

I'm a wonderful painter, you must have heard of me,
Marvel at my amazing artistic ability!
With palette, brush and paints in hand,
I'll be the most famous artist in the land!

The Magical Crafts Fairies can't stop me,
I'll steal their magic and then you'll see
That everyone, whatever the cost,
Will want a painting by Jack Frost!

Contents

Camp Breakfast   9

Art in the Garden   19

An A-Maze-ing Artist   31

Litter Louts   41

Living Drawings   53

Vivid Imaginations   61

Camp Breakfast

"I think that Rainspell Island is my favourite place in the whole world!" said Kirsty Tate, twirling on the spot.

Her best friend Rachel Walker jumped up and took Kirsty's hands. They spun around in a circle until they fell down on the grass, dizzy and happy. It was springtime, and the campsite meadow was full of daisies and buttercups.

"The sun always shines on Rainspell Island," Rachel said, laughing.

Rainspell Island was the place where Rachel and Kirsty had first become friends, and where they began their adventures with the fairies. Now they were back there again with their families for Crafts Week.

Every day, the girls could take different classes in all sorts of arts and crafts, from painting to making jewellery. On the final day there was going to be an exhibition and competition, with prizes! Everyone who had taken part in Crafts Week could enter whatever they had made, with the chance to win something. Rachel and Kirsty were really looking forward to it.

"Breakfast!" called Mrs Walker.

The girls raced back to the ten...
the Walkers were staying for their
holiday. Mr and Mrs Walker were sitt..g
outside the tent, cooking beans, sausages
and tomatoes on their camp stove.

"It's a beautiful morning," said Mr
Walker. "I bet your parents wish they
were camping too, Kirsty."

Mr and Mrs Tate were staying in a local Bed and Breakfast, but Kirsty and Rachel had decided to have a sleepover in the tent so that they could spend all their time together.

"So, girls, which crafts classes are you doing today?" asked Mrs Walker.

Today was the second day of Crafts Week, and there were lots of crafts that the girls wanted to try.

"We haven't decided yet," said Rachel, sitting down on a camp stool and holding out her plate for some breakfast.

"What do you think, Kirsty?"

Kirsty smiled and held out her own plate for breakfast.

"There are so many to choose from, I can't make up my mind," she said.

Mr and Mrs Walker started to talk about an exhibition they wanted to see, and Kirsty leaned closer to her best friend.

"I wonder if we'll meet another fairy today," she whispered.

"I hope so," Rachel replied in a low voice. "There are six magical objects still to find, and we don't know where to start looking!"

Yesterday, Kayla the Pottery Fairy had whisked them off to Fairyland for the grand opening of the fairies' Magical Crafts Week. Kirsty and Rachel had met the seven Magical Crafts Fairies, who showed them the magical objects they used to make sure everyone had fun doing arts and crafts.

The girls started to eat their breakfast, thinking about all the things that had happened in Fairyland the day before. While they were standing in a crowd of their fairy friends, King Oberon and Queen Titania had announced that they would be choosing the best crafts to decorate their Fairyland Palace. But at that moment, Jack Frost and his pesky goblins had thrown paint-filled balloons into the crowd, splattering the fairies with bright green paint. While everyone was distracted, Jack Frost and the goblins had snatched the magical objects from the Magical Crafts Fairies.

"I'm so glad that we managed to find Kayla's magical vase yesterday," said Kirsty quietly. "But we must find the rest of the magical objects, otherwise arts and crafts will be ruined, both in our world and in Fairyland."

"Jack Frost doesn't care about that," said Rachel. "He just wants to get his own way. Oh Kirsty, we have to stop him! What shall we do?"

Jack Frost had decided that he was the greatest artist ever, and he had stolen the objects to make sure no one tried to be better than him. They were hidden somewhere in the human world, so Kirsty and Rachel had offered to help the Magical Crafts Fairies to find them.

Kirsty took Rachel's hand and squeezed it.

"We just have to keep looking out for the magical objects," she said. "After all, Queen Titania does always say that we should wait for the magic to come to us."

Suddenly each of the girls felt a hand

on their shoulders, and Mr Walker leaned forward between them.

"What was that about magic?" he asked, raising his eyebrows.

Kirsty and Rachel exchanged worried looks. How much had Mr Walker heard?

Art in the Garden

"I'm glad that you think Crafts Week is magical," said Mr Walker.

Rachel and Kirsty let out sighs of relief. He hadn't realised that they were talking about the fairies!

"We're planning to go to an exhibition this morning," he went on, handing them a Crafts Week brochure. "A local artist called Sara Sketchley is showing a collection of her paintings at her house.

Why don't you come along with us?
She's holding a drawing class in her
garden, and you could join in."

"That sounds like a lovely thing to do
on a sunny day," said Rachel.

Kirsty nodded in agreement, so the
girls hurried into the tent to pack their
bags with the right equipment. They
picked out two sketchbooks and filled
their pencil cases with colouring
pencils, rubbers and pencil sharpeners.

Then they helped Mr and Mrs Walker wash and dry up the pans and plates from breakfast.

"Time to go to the exhibition," said Mrs Walker, checking her watch. "The drawing class starts in ten minutes."

They zipped up their tent and set off across the campsite meadow. Rachel and Kirsty raced each other to the entrance gate and then waited for Mr and Mrs Walker to catch them up.

"We must keep a lookout for goblins today," said Rachel. "I bet Jack Frost has ordered them to hide the fairies' magical objects."

Mr and Mrs Walker joined them and led the way down the lane to Sara Sketchley's house. It was a pretty little cottage with pink roses around the door, and honeysuckle trailing around the windows. The front garden had been turned into an outside gallery, with paintings hanging from the trees and propped up in the flowerbeds. Everywhere the girls looked they saw beautiful art.

"These roses look so real," said Kirsty, gazing at a painting that was dangling from an apple tree. "I feel as if I could reach out and touch them."

"Sara Sketchley obviously draws from life," said Mrs Walker, looking around at the flower-filled garden. "She must be a very keen gardener as well as a talented artist."

"I think her whole house must be an art gallery," said Rachel.

She pointed to a sign painted on a piece of driftwood.

More paintings this way ➡

The arrow was pointing into the house. "Shall we go inside?" said Mr Walker.

"Is it all right if Kirsty and I explore?" Rachel asked.

Sara Sketchley's garden was the size of a small park, and the girls were longing to look around.

"Of course," said Mrs Walker. "We'll see you later."

Rachel and Kirsty found the garden full of wonderful secrets waiting to be discovered. They saw a clear stream gurgling across the garden, over a watermill and under an old stone bridge.

They spotted a sign pointing the way
to a garden maze on the other side of
the bridge.

"That sounds brilliant," said Rachel,
remembering the other magical maze
on Rainspell Island where they had met
Fern the Green Fairy.

"Yes, I love mazes," Kirsty agreed.
"Shall we go?"

Rachel was about to agree
when she saw a group of
children following
a young woman to
a grassy spot beside
the bridge.

"I think that must be the start of the drawing class," she said. "We'll have to try out the maze later. Come on!"

They ran over to join the others, and took a seat on the grass close to the bridge. The young woman was standing beside an easel, and she smiled at them. She had bright-green eyes and brown curls that flowed over her shoulders. Her long skirt was decorated with a daisy-chain belt, and her feet were bare except for a silver ankle chain.

"Welcome to my drawing class, everyone," she said in a warm, rich voice. "It's wonderful to see so many people who are interested in drawing. I am passionate about art, and I believe that doing arts and crafts makes people feel calm and happy. So let's get started! Please take out your pencils and drawing pads. I'm going to show you how to draw a lifelike rose."

Kirsty opened her art bag and put her hand inside. Then she let out a little cry of surprise.

"There's something inside my bag!" she whispered to Rachel. "I felt it fluttering against my hand."

Rachel just smiled.

"It wasn't some*thing*, it was some*one*," she said. "Look!"

Annabelle the Drawing Fairy was smiling at them over the edge of Kirsty's art bag.

An A-Maze-ing Artist

Annabelle was wearing a pretty tie-dye top and cropped blue jeans. Her blonde hair was shining in the sunlight.

"Hello, Annabelle!" whispered Rachel, feeling very excited. "What are you doing here?"

"I've come to ask you to help me find my magical pencil sharpener," Annabelle said in a silvery voice. "Without it, drawings everywhere will be ruined."

"Of course we'll help," said Kirsty.

"Thank you!" said Annabelle, ducking down into the art bag again.

"Look carefully at the roses growing all around you," said Sara Sketchley. "I'm going to draw one first, and then I'd like you to have a go."

Sara picked up a pencil and turned to the paper that was clipped to her easel. As soon as she pressed the pencil against the paper, the point broke.

"Oops," said Sara with a little laugh. "That happens sometimes!"

She picked up another pencil, but this

one snapped in half. Sara frowned and picked up a third pencil.

"You start with delicate, light pencil strokes," she said.

She drew a line on the paper, but it wasn't gentle or soft. It was a thick, angry slash that almost ripped the paper. Sara gasped.

"I'm sorry, everyone," she said. "I don't know what's the matter with me today!"

Kirsty and Rachel exchanged a secret glance. They both knew that it must have something to do with the missing magical pencil sharpener.

"I'm going to go and fetch a better pencil," said Sara. "Please start drawing your own lifelike sketches while you wait."

Rachel and Kirsty felt sorry for Sara Sketchley. Jack Frost was spoiling her art class, and they had no idea how to stop him. Rachel picked up a pencil and then put it down again.

"I can't concentrate on drawing," she said. "Let's see how the others are doing."

She stood up and strolled around the grassy area, looking at the pictures the other children were drawing. When she had seen two or three, she beckoned to Kirsty.

"Come and see these," she said in a low voice.

34

Kirsty picked up her art bag and followed Rachel. The other children were drawing roses, but their pictures were all dreadful. The roses looked ugly, with huge thorns and withered petals.

"These look nothing like the roses," said Kirsty. "They're all horrible."

"All except that one," said Rachel.

She nodded over to a boy in green dungarees and a beret, who was drawing the watermill. His picture was very good. It was so realistic that the girls felt as if they could almost hear the stream gurgling.

Annabelle peeped out of the art bag, and just at that moment the boy looked up from his sketchpad. Annabelle drew in her breath sharply, and Rachel grabbed Kirsty's hand. The boy had a long, green nose.

36

"He's a goblin!" said Kirsty in a shocked voice.

"That's why he's drawing so well," said Annabelle. "He must have my magical pencil sharpener!"

The goblin glanced over at the girls, and his beady eyes spotted Annabelle straight away. He jumped up and his easel fell over as he darted towards the bridge.

"Catch him!" cried Annabelle. "We have to stop him!"

Rachel and Kirsty raced after him. He scampered over the bridge and into the garden maze. The girls followed, their feet clattering on the little wooden bridge. But when they ran into the maze, the goblin had disappeared. High hedges surrounded them. The girls reached a crossway and stopped.

"Which way?" asked Kirsty, glancing left and right.

"Quick, Annabelle, change us into fairies!" said Rachel. "If we can fly above the hedges, we can spot him!"

Annabelle fluttered out of the art bag and waved her wand. Instantly, the girls felt a tingling in their shoulders, and gossamer wings appeared as they shrank to fairy size. The maze hedges seemed twenty times bigger, but Annabelle, Rachel and Kirsty zoomed into the air and hovered above them.

"I see him!" cried Annabelle. "He's over there!"

"No, this way!" said Rachel, pointing in the opposite direction.

Kirsty looked down and groaned.

"Oh no! There are four goblins in the maze!" she exclaimed.

Litter Louts

As the girls watched, the goblins joined
together at the far side of the maze.
One of them had a sketchbook, and was
tearing pages out of it. He crumpled
them up and tossed them at the other
goblins, who squawked with laughter
and threw them around. Balls of
screwed-up paper were landing on the
ground and even on top of the hedges.

"How dare they?" Rachel burst out.

She zoomed down towards the goblins and hovered in front of them.

"Stop this now!" she demanded. "You're wasting paper and you're making the maze all messy."

"Be quiet, silly fairy!" shouted the goblin with the sketchpad. "Mind your own business."

"This *is* our business," said Kirsty, flying down to hover beside her best friend. "You're being litterbugs, and it's everyone's job to keep the environment tidy."

A tall goblin capered around with his fingers in his ears.

"I can't hear you!" he squawked in a singsong voice. "I can't hear you!"

Just then, Kirsty saw a small, plump goblin throw something the size of a pencil sharpener into the air. Could it be Annabelle's magical object? She swooped down as it flew up, and caught it in her outstretched hand.

"Is it my pencil sharpener?" asked Annabelle, darting down to join Kirsty.

"No," said Kirsty with a sigh.

She held out her hand and showed Annabelle an ordinary rubber.

"I don't think these goblins have the magical pencil sharpener," said Rachel. "They're just messing around and causing trouble."

"You're right," said Kirsty. "If they *did* have it, they'd be using its magic to draw beautiful pictures, like the first goblin."

"We have to keep looking," said Rachel. "He's somewhere in this maze."

"Let's spread out," suggested Annabelle. "If we fly low over the hedges, we'll find him eventually."

The three fairies flew above the maze, peering down among the dark green hedges. It was hard to see because the bright sunshine made some dark shadows. But at last Rachel spotted another goblin in the very centre of the maze. He was sitting on a stone in

a rock garden, drawing a picture of a
nearby garden gnome.

Rachel beckoned to Kirsty and
Annabelle.

"It's him!" she said as they fluttered
towards her. "Look, he's drawing
again – I think he must have the magic
pencil sharpener."

"But where is it?" asked Kirsty.

"And how can we get it back from
him?" added Annabelle.

They all thought hard, and then

Kirsty's eyes sparkled.

"I've got an idea," she said. "But if this is going to work, Rachel and I will need to be human-sized again."

They all flew down and landed on the cool ground in the shadow of a hedge. Then Annabelle tapped the girls with her wand, and they were transformed into humans again. Rachel looked at Kirsty

with an excited and hopeful expression.

"What's the plan?" she asked.

"I think we should try to get the goblin to draw our pictures," said Kirsty. "If we can get close to him, we might get a chance to take back Annabelle's magical pencil sharpener."

Annabelle clapped her hands together, and Rachel gave her best friend a smile.

"That's a really good idea, Kirsty," she said. "Goblins are so vain, we might be able to distract him for long enough to find the pencil sharpener."

Annabelle flew into

Rachel's pocket and tucked herself down
out of sight. Then Rachel and Kirsty
linked arms and walked around the
corner into the centre of the maze.

"We found it!" said Rachel in a loud
voice. "We've reached the centre of the
maze. Oh, look – there's someone here
before us!"

The goblin glanced up and spotted

them standing there.

"It's that wonderful artist we saw earlier," said Kirsty, making sure that the goblin could hear her. "Let's go and see what he's drawing now."

They walked over to the goblin, who had almost finished his picture of the gnome. He jumped up and stood in front of his easel, folding his arms across his chest.

"Go away!" he snapped. "I don't speak to friends of that pesky fairy."

"What do you mean?" said Rachel with a laugh. "How could we be friends with a fairy when there's no such thing?"

Kirsty laughed too and leaned forward to look at the painting.

"You're a really good artist," she said. "You've made that gnome so lifelike. I bet you can draw people really well too."

The goblin gave a smug little smile.

"I'm the best artist you've ever met," he said. "I'm even better than that Sara Sketchley."

"Can you draw us?" Kirsty asked.

"Oh that would be wonderful," Rachel exclaimed, clapping her hands together. "Please say yes!"

Living Drawings

The goblin artist puffed out his chest.

"I can draw anything!" he said.
"Drawing you two will be easy-peasy."

He flipped over his drawing pad to a
new page and turned the easel to face
the girls. The girls posed arm in arm and
the goblin's pencil flew across the paper.

It only seemed to take a few moments, and then the goblin signed his picture with a flourish and turned it around to show the girls.

Rachel and Kirsty gasped. They knew it was the magic of the pencil sharpener, but the picture was astonishingly good. It was almost like looking in a mirror.

"You must be a great artist," said Rachel. "I wish I could draw like that! Oh, would you teach us how to draw?"

"We could practise by drawing you," Kirsty suggested. "You've got such an… interesting face."

"I expect lots of artists want to paint you," Rachel added. "You're so rugged and…um… handsome."

The goblin strutted up and down in front of them and then struck a pose,

standing with one foot up
on a large stone.

"Yes, draw me,"
he said. "Try to
capture my good
looks and charm."

Kirsty pulled
out a pencil and
secretly broke off
the point. Then
she held it up.

"Oh no, my pencil's
broken," she said.

Rachel quickly broke off the tip of her
pencil as well.

"Mine too," she said with a groan.
"And I don't have a pencil sharpener."

"Neither do I," said Kirsty, pretending
to search through her pencil case.

55

The goblin looked upset. He had been feeling quite excited about having his picture drawn.

"Hurry up!" he snarled. "Get on with it."

"Do you have a pencil sharpener we could use?" Kirsty asked. "If we can't find one, we won't be able to draw you!"

The goblin gazed at them, and the girls felt their hearts pounding. Would their plan work? Had they managed to fool the goblin?

"Don't you have other pencils you can use?" asked the goblin.

Rachel and Kirsty exchanged glances. He sounded very suspicious. But they couldn't tell a lie – they had pencil cases full of other pencils! The goblin took a step towards them, and then his face crumpled into a sneer.

"I know you!" he screeched. "I never forget a face! You were with that do-gooder fairy earlier."

He blew a loud raspberry and then dashed away from them.

57

"Annabelle, we need some drawings of hedges, quickly!" cried Rachel.

Annabelle zoomed into the air and flicked her wand. A life-size drawing of a hedge dropped down in front of the goblin. He turned in the opposite direction, and another hedge drawing dropped in front of him. He thought that the hedges were real! Believing that his way was blocked, he let out a loud wail.

"I'm trapped!" he yelled. "Let me out! I don't like this maze any more!"

"Give Annabelle's magic pencil sharpener back," called Kirsty. "Then we'll let you out."

"No way!" the goblin shouted. "Jack Frost told me to keep it away from you interfering fairies!"

"Then you'll just have to stay in the maze," said Kirsty.

"I don't like it!" the goblin cried out. "I'm hungry! I'm thirsty! I want to go to the toilet!"

"All you have to do is give Annabelle's magic pencil sharpener back," said Rachel. "It's rightfully hers — it doesn't belong to you."

High above them, Annabelle gave a cry of excitement.

"He's opening his pencil case!" she called out.

Vivid Imaginations

Peeping around the edge of the paper hedge, Rachel and Kirsty saw the goblin take a shimmering silver pencil sharpener out of his pencil case. He squinted angrily up at Annabelle.

"Here, come and take it," he said in a cross voice. "And may you never have a day's luck with it! You rotten fairies spoil everything."

Annabelle fluttered down and took the exquisite pencil sharpener from the goblin's bony grasp. It immediately shrank to fairy size, and the magical hedge drawings vanished in a puff of fairy glitter. Rachel and Kirsty hugged each other, and Annabelle gave a little twirl in midair. The goblin shuffled back to the picture of the gnome that he had been drawing. He picked up his pencil and tried to finish the drawing, but all his lines were squiggly. The gnome in his picture started to look very skinny and bony.

The other goblins appeared from inside the maze, and walked up to him. They didn't notice Kirsty and Rachel standing at the side.

"That's a rubbish picture," said one of them scornfully.

"What do you know about drawing?" snorted the goblin artist.

"Much more than you, judging by your drawing," sniggered another goblin.

"Why have all the pages been returned to my sketchbook?" asked a third goblin. "I crumpled half of them up and now they're all as good as new."

"That's because dropping litter is wrong," said Rachel, stepping out of the shadow of the hedge. "You goblins should learn about taking care of the world around you. When Annabelle got her magical pencil sharpener back, she used her magic to tidy up the naughty mess you made."

The other goblins ignored Rachel and whirled around to glare at the goblin artist.

"You idiot!" the tall goblin shrieked. "How could you let the fairy get her magical object back? Jack Frost is going to send us to the dungeons for this again!"

"I was STUCK!" the goblin artist screeched in anger.

"Never mind that," said the plumper goblin. "What are we going to tell Jack Frost?"

The goblins all sat down on differently-sized stones in the rock garden and began to think.

Rachel and Kirsty giggled as Annabelle flew over to them.

"Follow me and I'll lead you through the maze to the exit," she said.

Rachel and Kirsty left the goblins arguing about how to tell Jack Frost the terrible news. They kept their eyes on Annabelle, and she guided them all the way to the exit. There, she fluttered down beside them. Her magic pencil sharpener was clutched in her hand.

"I'm not letting this out of my sight," she said with a big smile. "Girls, you have saved drawings all over the world. Thank you so much for helping me. Without you, I'm sure Jack Frost's goblins would still have my magical object."

"We were pleased to help," said
Rachel honestly.

"Hopefully we can do the same for the
other missing objects," Kirsty added.

"I'll tell the other Magical Crafts
Fairies how wonderful you are,"
said Annabelle. "Goodbye, and thank
you again!"

As the girls raised their hands to wave
goodbye, Annabelle disappeared in a
shower of fairy sparkles.

"Come on," said Kirsty. "Let's get back
to the drawing class."

Hand in hand, the girls ran back
across the bridge to the main part of the
garden. Sara Sketchley was standing
among the other children, holding up a
finished picture of a beautiful rose.

"Now you've seen me drawing, I want

to see what you can do," she was saying. "I'd like you to draw the most beautiful thing you can think of from your own imagination. It can be a person or a place. It can be real or fantasy. Just have fun!"

Rachel and Kirsty exchanged a happy smile as they rejoined the class. They knew exactly what they were going to draw! They took out their pencils and sketchbooks.

"My pencil is as good as new!" whispered Rachel. "Look!"

"Mine too," said Kirsty, pressing her finger to the sharp point of her pencil. "Thank you, Annabelle!"

The girls were both engrossed in their drawings when they heard a familiar voice.

"Everyone seems to be very hard at work here!"

The girls looked up and saw Artemis Johnson, the organiser of Crafts Week. She was walking towards Sara Sketchley, with Mr and Mrs Walker.

"Hello, Artie," said Sara with a smile. "Yes, everyone's very busy. Let's have a look at how you're all getting on."

She led Artie and Mr and Mrs Walker around the little group. When they reached Rachel and Kirsty, Sara put a hand on each of their shoulders.

"These are very interesting," she said. "You girls are very talented! Kirsty's picture of a magic fairy land is so realistic that I can imagine being there! And Rachel, your fairy is so lifelike that I'm half expecting her to flutter out of the paper and cast a spell!"

"What vivid imaginations," said Artie. "I can't wait for the exhibition at the end of the week!"

Mr and Mrs Walker beamed with pride. Kirsty and Rachel reached out their hands to each other and linked their little fingers in their secret sign of friendship. Kirsty had drawn the Fairyland Palace, which she had visited many times. Rachel had drawn a picture of Annabelle. They were simply drawing from real life!

As the grown-ups moved away, the girls whispered to each other about their magical morning.

"Do you think we'll have another adventure tomorrow?" asked Kirsty.

Rachel looked at her best friend and smiled happily.

"I'm sure we will!" she said.

The End

Now it's time for Kirsty and Rachel to help...

Zadie the Sewing Fairy

Read on for a sneak peek...

"It's another magical morning, Kirsty," Rachel said, gazing out of the window of Mimosa Cottage. Although it was still quite early, the sun was already shining, and Rainspell Island looked green and beautiful with the morning light glinting on the sea.

"Do you mean the weather, or our adventures with the Magical Crafts Fairies?" Kirsty asked, her eyes twinkling. They'd arrived on Rainspell two days ago and the girls were taking it in turns to spend one night in Kirsty's quaint little attic bedroom at the B&B with the

Tates, and then one night with Rachel's parents at a nearby campsite. The girls loved holidaying on Rainspell Island because it was where they'd first become friends with the fairies.

"A little bit of both!" Rachel replied. "Wasn't it *mean* of Jack Frost to steal all the fairies' magical objects?"

Read Zadie the Sewing Fairy to find out what adventures are in store for Kirsty and Rachel!

RAINBOW magic

Join in the magic online by signing up to the Rainbow Magic fan club!

Sign up today at:
www.rainbowmagicbooks.co.uk

Meet the
Magical Crafts Fairies

Jack Frost has stolen the Magical Crafts Fairies' special objects. Can Kirsty and Rachel help get them back before Rainspell Island's Crafts Week is ruined?

www.rainbowmagicbooks.co.uk

Competition!

The Magical Crafts Fairies have created a special
competition just for you!
In the back of each book in the Magical Crafts series there
will be a question for you to answer.
First you need to collect the answer from the back
of each book in the series.
Once you have all the answers, take the first letter from
each one and arrange them to spell a secret word!
When you have the answer, go online and enter!

**Naughty Jack Frost and his goblins
live in a castle made of this...**

_ _ _

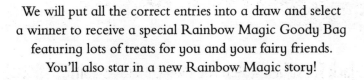

We will put all the correct entries into a draw and select
a winner to receive a special Rainbow Magic Goody Bag
featuring lots of treats for you and your fairy friends.
You'll also star in a new Rainbow Magic story!

Enter online now at www.rainbowmagicbooks.co.uk

Have you read them all?

The Rainbow Fairies
1. Ruby the Red Fairy ☐
2. Amber the Orange Fairy ☐
3. Saffron the Yellow Fairy ☐
4. Fern the Green Fairy ☐
5. Sky the Blue Fairy ☐
6. Izzy the Indigo Fairy ☐
7. Heather the Violet Fairy ☐

The Weather Fairies
8. Crystal the Snow Fairy ☐
9. Abigail the Breeze Fairy ☐
10. Pearl the Cloud Fairy ☐
11. Goldie the Sunshine Fairy ☐
12. Evie the Mist Fairy ☐
13. Storm the Lightning Fairy ☐
14. Hayley the Rain Fairy ☐

The Party Fairies
15. Cherry the Cake Fairy ☐
16. Melodie the Music Fairy ☐
17. Grace the Glitter Fairy ☐
18. Honey the Sweet Fairy ☐
19. Polly the Party Fun Fairy ☐
20. Phoebe the Fashion Fairy ☐
21. Jasmine the Present Fairy ☐

The Jewel Fairies
22. India the Moonstone Fairy ☐
23. Scarlett the Garnet Fairy ☐
24. Emily the Emerald Fairy ☐
25. Chloe the Topaz Fairy ☐
26. Amy the Amethyst Fairy ☐
27. Sophie the Sapphire Fairy ☐
28. Lucy the Diamond Fairy ☐

The Pet Keeper Fairies
29. Katie the Kitten Fairy ☐
30. Bella the Bunny Fairy ☐
31. Georgia the Guinea Pig Fairy ☐
32. Lauren the Puppy Fairy ☐
33. Harriet the Hamster Fairy ☐
34. Molly the Goldfish Fairy ☐
35. Penny the Pony Fairy ☐

The Fun Day Fairies
36. Megan the Monday Fairy
37. Tallulah the Tuesday Fairy
38. Willow the Wednesday Fairy
39. Thea the Thursday Fairy
40. Freya the Friday Fairy
41. Sienna the Saturday Fairy
42. Sarah the Sunday Fairy

The Petal Fairies
43. Tia the Tulip Fairy
44. Pippa the Poppy Fairy
45. Louise the Lily Fairy
46. Charlotte the Sunflower Fairy
47. Olivia the Orchid Fairy
48. Danielle the Daisy Fairy
49. Ella the Rose Fairy

The Dance Fairies
50. Bethany the Ballet Fairy
51. Jade the Disco Fairy
52. Rebecca the Rock'n'Roll Fairy
53. Tasha the Tap Dance Fairy
54. Jessica the Jazz Fairy
55. Saskia the Salsa Fairy
56. Imogen the Ice Dance Fairy

The Sporty Fairies
57. Helena the Horseriding Fairy
58. Francesca the Football Fairy
59. Zoe the Skating Fairy
60. Naomi the Netball Fairy
61. Samantha the Swimming Fairy
62. Alice the Tennis Fairy
63. Gemma the Gymnastics Fairy

The Music Fairies
64. Poppy the Piano Fairy
65. Ellie the Guitar Fairy
66. Fiona the Flute Fairy
67. Danni the Drum Fairy
68. Maya the Harp Fairy
69. Victoria the Violin Fairy
70. Sadie the Saxophone Fairy

The Magical Animal Fairies
71. Ashley the Dragon Fairy ☐
72. Lara the Black Cat Fairy ☐
73. Erin the Firebird Fairy ☐
74. Rihanna the Seahorse Fairy ☐
75. Sophia the Snow Swan Fairy ☐
76. Leona the Unicorn Fairy ☐
77. Caitlin the Ice Bear Fairy ☐

The Green Fairies
78. Nicole the Beach Fairy ☐
79. Isabella the Air Fairy ☐
80. Edie the Garden Fairy ☐
81. Coral the Reef Fairy ☐
82. Lily the Rainforest Fairy ☐
83. Carrie the Snow Cap Fairy ☐
84. Milly the River Fairy ☐

The Ocean Fairies
85. Ally the Dolphin Fairy ☐
86. Amelie the Seal Fairy ☐
87. Pia the Penguin Fairy ☐
88. Tess the Sea Turtle Fairy ☐
89. Stephanie the Starfish Fairy ☐
90. Whitney the Whale Fairy ☐
91. Courtney the Clownfish Fairy ☐

The Twilight Fairies
92. Ava the Sunset Fairy ☐
93. Lexi the Firefly Fairy ☐
94. Zara the Starlight Fairy ☐
95. Morgan the Midnight Fairy ☐
96. Yasmin the Night Owl Fairy ☐
97. Maisie the Moonbeam Fairy ☐
98. Sabrina the Sweet Dreams Fairy ☐

The Showtime Fairies
99. Madison the Magic Show Fairy ☐
100. Leah the Theatre Fairy ☐
101. Alesha the Acrobat Fairy ☐
102. Darcey the Dance Diva Fairy ☐
103. Taylor the Talent Show Fairy ☐
104. Amelia the Singing Fairy ☐
105. Isla the Ice Star Fairy ☐

The Princess Fairies
106. Honor the Happy Days Fairy ☐
107. Demi the Dressing-Up Fairy ☐
108. Anya the Cuddly Creatures Fairy ☐
109. Elisa the Adventure Fairy ☐
110. Lizzie the Sweet Treats Fairy ☐
111. Maddie the Playtime Fairy ☐
112. Eva the Enchanted Ball Fairy ☐

The Pop Star Fairies
113. Jessie the Lyrics Fairy ☐
114. Adele the Singing Coach Fairy ☐
115. Vanessa the Dance Steps Fairy ☐
116. Miley the Stylist Fairy ☐
117. Frankie the Make-Up Fairy ☐
118. Rochelle the Star Spotter Fairy ☐
119. Una the Concert Fairy ☐

The Fashion Fairies
120. Miranda the Beauty Fairy ☐
121. Claudia the Accessories Fairy ☐
122. Tyra the Dress Designer Fairy ☐
123. Alexa the Fashion Reporter Fairy ☐
124. Matilda the Hair Stylist Fairy ☐
125. Brooke the Photographer Fairy ☐
126. Lola the Fashion Fairy ☐

The Sweet Fairies
127. Lottie the Lollipop Fairy ☐
128. Esme the Ice Cream Fairy ☐
129. Coco the Cupcake Fairy ☐
130. Clara the Chocolate Fairy ☐
131. Madeleine the Cookie Fairy ☐
132. Layla the Candyfloss Fairy ☐
133. Nina the Birthday Cake Fairy ☐

The Baby Animal Rescue Fairies
134. Mae the Panda Fairy ☐
135. Kitty the Tiger Fairy ☐
136. Mara the Meerkat Fairy ☐
137. Savannah the Zebra Fairy ☐
138. Kimberley the Koala Fairy ☐
139. Rosie the Honey Bear Fairy ☐
140. Anna the Arctic Fox Fairy ☐

The Magical Crafts Fairies
141. Kayla the Pottery Fairy ☐
142. Annabelle the Drawing Fairy ☐
143. Zadie the Sewing Fairy ☐
144. Josie the Jewellery-Making Fairy ☐
145. Violet the Painting Fairy ☐
146. Libby the Story-Writing Fairy ☐
147. Roxie the Baking Fairy ☐

There's a book of fairy fun for everyone!

www.rainbowmagicbooks.co.uk

Lila & Myla the Twins Fairies

Meet Lila and Myla the Twins Fairies!
Can the fairies stop Jack Frost before he uses
their magic to create his very own twin?

www.rainbowmagicbooks.co.uk